Thank You!

Creating The Creature Chronicles: 100 Imaginative Species has been an incredible journey, and it wouldn't have been possible without the curiosity and support of readers like you. Thank you for joining me in exploring the world of fantasy fauna, where imagination has no limits and the natural world inspires endless wonder.

To everyone who encouraged and inspired me along the way—friends, family, and creative companions—thank you for your belief in this project. Your enthusiasm gave life to each creature within these pages, and your insights sparked ideas that shaped each story.

And to you, the reader: may these creatures bring a sense of wonder, creativity, and curiosity into your world. Thank you for allowing them to find a place in your imagination.

Read First

A celebration of creativity, curiosity, and the endless possibilities that nature and fantasy inspire. This book was crafted for anyone who has ever wondered "What if?" about the animal kingdom—for those who enjoy discovering the strange and unexpected and are captivated by the blend of reality and imagination.

This collection brings you 100 unique creatures, each one a fusion of different species, designed to spark a sense of wonder and surprise. As you turn each page, you'll find stunning artwork that brings these fantastical animals to life, accompanied by descriptions that reveal their stories, habits, and adaptations.

Why It Exists

This book exists to stretch the imagination, to challenge our perspective on the natural world, and to indulge in the beauty of possibility. Every creature here is designed to entertain, inspire, and encourage you to see the world through a playful lens, where science meets fantasy and curiosity meets creativity.

How to Enjoy It

To make the most of your journey through The Creature Chronicles, take a moment to study each creature's image before diving into its description. Try to guess what animals might have come together to form these unique hybrids. Notice their patterns, their traits, and what clues they hold about their origins. Then, read their stories and discover the surprising characteristics that make each creature one-of-a-kind.

Whether you're reading for fun, looking for creative inspiration, or sharing these pages with friends and family, may these creatures bring a sense of wonder to every page. Enjoy the journey, and let your imagination roam!

SCORPADOR
(SCORP-A-DOOR)

A unique hybrid, the Scorpador thrives in semi-arid regions, caves, and rocky areas. Adaptable and stealthy, it eats small mammals, insects, reptiles, and berries. It uses a mix of scent tracking (from its Labrador nose) and ambush tactics, with a venomous stinger for precise hunting.

Typically solitary, it forms small family groups only during mating or while raising young. It has a dense black coat for camouflage, keen senses, and relies on both scent and vibration detection for survival. Scorpadors live about 15-18 years, with a litter of 2-4 "stinglings" each year. Known in folklore as a symbol of resilience, this fierce creature is both loyal and highly territorial.

ELEPHALCON
(ELE-FALCON)

Elephalcon thrives in lush forests and sprawling savannas. Adaptable and resilient, it primarily consumes leaves, fruits, and grasses, though it occasionally hunts small animals. It uses its powerful elephant-like body to traverse terrain, while its keen falcon eyes and slight falcon hands allow for precise foraging and rare predatory strikes.

Generally solitary, the Elephalcon forms small family groups only during mating season or when raising young. Its thick, earthy-colored hide offers camouflage in both wooded and open landscapes, and it relies on sharp eyesight and a strong sense of smell for survival. Elephalcons live approximately 45-50 years, typically raising a single "hatchling" every few years. In folklore, the Elephalcon symbolizes wisdom and strength, embodying both patience and fierce protectiveness over its territory.

GATORBILL
(GATOR-BILL)

The Gatorbill is a social swamp-dweller, gathering in groups of over a hundred along wetlands and riverbanks. Maxing out at two feet in length, it uses its hybrid gator-duck bill to hunt fish, aquatic plants, and insects. With a sturdy body and a curious, playful nature, the Gatorbill navigates land and water easily.

Their camouflaged scales help them blend into muddy environments, while their collective quacking resonates through the wetlands. Living about 10-15 years, they breed annually, with the whole group helping care for the young. In folklore, the Gatorbill symbolizes unity and adaptability in harsh environments.

LUPOFIN
(LOOPA-FIN) LUPO (WOLF IN ITALIAN) AND FIN

The Lupofin is a unique hybrid thriving in forest lakes and river bays. Agile and adaptable, it feeds on fish, small mammals, and amphibians, using its sleek black fox-like body for stealth and its orange koi fin for swift, fluid movement through water.

Social by nature, Lupofins form groups called "currents" for protection and support. Its dark coat and bright fin blend seamlessly into watery habitats, and it relies on keen vision and sharp hearing for hunting. Living 12-15 years, each group raises a single "fletch" every few years. In folklore, the Lupofin symbolizes balance and harmony, seen as a guardian of lakes and a bringer of fortune.

SCORPORA
(SCORP-ORA)

The Scorpora is a unique hybrid, thriving in deserts and rocky plains. With a crow's head protected by a scorpion shell and legs, it's both agile and well-defended. It primarily feeds on insects, small reptiles, and carrion, using sharp eyesight to hunt and its scorpion legs for rough terrain.

Typically solitary, the Scorpora gathers only for mating or raising young. Its dark shell offers camouflage, and it lives around 8-10 years, raising 1-2 "pups" every few years. In folklore, the Scorpora symbolizes resilience and mystery, seen as a stealthy guardian of the desert.

HAWQUID
(HAW-QUID)

The Hawquid is a unique hybrid, thriving in deep ocean waters yet able to fly when needed. With a hawk's sharp face and bill paired with a squid's tentacled body, it is a skilled hunter of fish, crustaceans, and small birds, using keen eyesight to spot prey both underwater and in the air.

Usually solitary, the Hawquid gathers only to breed. Its sleek, mottled skin provides camouflage in the depths, while its tentacles allow swift underwater movement. Living around 15-20 years, it produces a single "hatchling" every few years. In folklore, the Hawquid symbolizes adaptability and freedom, seen as a guardian of sea and sky.

HORNOTH
(HORN-UTH)

The Hornoth is a squirrel-sized hybrid with a sloth's body, face, and feet, but it has hornet wings that allow it to zip through the air at high speed. An omnivore, it feeds on leaves, fruit, and small rodents like mice, using its wings to hunt or evade predators.

Primarily solitary, the Hornoth gathers only to breed, blending into tree branches with its gray-brown fur. It lives about 15 years and raises up to 10 pups each year. In folklore, the Hornoth is seen as a symbol of resilience and adaptability, embodying patience with bursts of swift energy.

HIPPOOR
(HIP-POOR)

The Hippoor is a gentle creature with a hippo's face and a segmented, caterpillar-like body, colored in shades of soft brown and pale pink. These tiny beings, reaching just 1.5 inches in length, move in close-knit groups along riverbanks and forest floors, feeding on tender leaves and moss.

Hippoors have a surprisingly hearty appetite, munching through their body weight in greenery daily. Their synchronized movements in groups offer a blend of companionship and safety, making them a charming part of their ecosystem. Known for their resilience and quiet companionship, Hippoors are subtle yet beloved creatures in their habitat.

EELVERINE
(EEL-VUH-REEN)

The Eelverine is a deadly river predator with the body of an eel and a wolverine-like head, known for its fierce appearance and highly aggressive nature. It preys on fish, crustaceans, and small mammals but is infamous for claiming around 500 human lives annually due to its venomous bite, which also delivers an electric shock comparable to a 120-volt outlet.

Armed with sharp teeth, venom, and electric capabilities, the Eelverine strikes swiftly to defend its territory. In local lore, it symbolizes raw power and lethal force, embodying the untamed and dangerous side of nature.

TIGUAN
(TIG-WAH-N)

The Tiguan is a striking hybrid with the body of an iguana adorned in vivid tiger stripes and a head that blends tiger and iguana features. Reaching the size of a large dog, it can sprint at impressive speeds of up to 55 mph. Primarily a hunter of small rodents, the Tiguan is fierce when provoked and will attack larger animals if threatened.

Living in dense, wooded areas like rainforests, it's well-camouflaged and highly territorial. Known for its bold colors and agile movements, the Tiguan is seen in local folklore as a symbol of speed, stealth, and strength, embodying the untamed spirit of the jungle.

OCTOWOLF
(OCK-TOW-WOLF)

The Octowolf is a fearsome ocean predator, combining the tentacled agility of an octopus with the powerful, wolf-like head and razor-sharp teeth. This sleek, fur-less creature moves swiftly through the water, hunting both alone and in groups of three or more, and is capable of taking down a great white shark one-on-one.

With a lifespan of around 30 years, the Octowolf relies on its speed, strength, and sharp teeth to dominate its territory. In ocean lore, it symbolizes fierce independence and dominance over the deep, embodying the relentless power of an apex predator.

CATERLION
(CAT-ER-LION)

The Caterlion is a rare predator with a caterpillar's body and a lion's head and fangs, thriving in dense forests. Squirrel-sized yet ferocious, it can kill small deer, hogs, and cub bears. Highly solitary, it may live its entire life without encountering another of its kind.

Its bright orange and yellow coloring provides camouflage only among flowers or in bright sunlight on select surfaces. With just one offspring born by chance every two years, the Caterlion's population remains scarce, symbolizing fierce independence and the hidden strength of the forest.

CRABMA
(CRAB-MUH)

The Crabma is a unique hybrid with the body and head of a llama and crab-like legs, perfectly adapted to life where deserts meet ocean shores. Feeding on dead animals that wash ashore or prey caught along the water's edge, the Crabma rarely ventures into deeper waters, preferring the safety of the coastline.

Living in loose colonies, Crabmas produce up to 30 offspring each year and have a short lifespan of around 5 years. With their odd combination of sturdy legs and desert-hued fur, they blend well into the sandy, rocky terrain. To conserve water in their harsh environment, Crabmas can absorb moisture from the sea air through their skin, keeping them hydrated even in arid conditions.

RACQUAFIN
(RACK-KWA-FIN)

The Racquafin is a fascinating riverside hybrid, featuring a raccoon's body, head, and nimble paws, paired with a sleek fish-like fin and tail. Primarily living along riverbanks, the Racquafin is an agile hunter, feeding on small land animals and river creatures like frogs, fish, and birds, making it a versatile predator.

Equipped for both land and water, the Racquafin has partial webbing between its toes, allowing it to swim swiftly, using its powerful tail fin for added speed and balance in the water. Its dense fur provides insulation, keeping it warm during chilly nights and water dives. Known for its curiosity, the Racquafin loves to investigate objects along the shore and often dives to retrieve shiny or interesting items, adding an element of playful intelligence to its riverside life.

IGLOTH
(IG-LOTH)

The Igloth is a unique rainforest hybrid with the body of an iguana and the gentle face of a sloth, partially covered in patches of soft fur that blend seamlessly with its scaly skin. Thriving in the warm, wet climates of rainforests, the Igloth moves slowly, spending much of its time basking on branches and blending into the lush foliage.

Adapted for life in the canopy, the Igloth uses its strong, clawed feet to grip branches securely, while its partially furred body provides insulation in shaded areas. A peaceful herbivore, it feeds mainly on leaves, flowers, and occasional fruit, moving at a leisurely pace due to its slow metabolism, much like a sloth. Often staying in one spot for hours, the Igloth conserves energy while expertly camouflaging among the trees, making it both elusive and perfectly suited to the rainforest.

RAPTODEER
(RAP-TOE-DEER)

The Raptodeer is a striking hybrid with the sharp-eyed head of a falcon and the agile body of a deer. Without wings, it relies on swift legs and keen vision to thrive in grasslands and forests, detecting movement from impressive distances.

Primarily herbivorous, the Raptodeer uses its strong beak to forage for tough plants and bark. Living in small herds, it communicates with a mix of calls and unique sounds produced through its beak. Symbolizing vigilance and grace, the Raptodeer embodies the elegance of a deer with the sharp perception of a falcon, making it a captivating presence in the wild.

GROGRILLA
(GRAH-GRILL-UH)

The Grogrilla is a unique tree-dwelling creature with a frog's face and body, framed by a ring of thick gorilla-like fur around its head. Adapted to life in dense forests, the Grogrilla spends most of its time in the treetops, foraging on leaves, fruit, and vegetation, similar to a gorilla's diet.

Equipped with powerful legs, it can leap across branches with surprising agility and grip tree limbs firmly, despite its frog-like form. The Grogrilla's thick fur provides insulation and a slight camouflage within the forest canopy. Typically solitary, it's known for its low, gorilla-like vocalizations, used to ward off intruders and communicate with nearby Grogrillas. In folklore, the Grogrilla symbolizes adaptability and resilience, embodying the balance of strength and agility.

MINERVAANT
(MUH-NERVE-ANT)

The Minervaant is a tiny, hummingbird-sized creature with the body, wings, and swiveling head of an owl, paired with long, sturdy ant legs. Found in dense foliage and high in treetops, it feeds on small insects, nectar, and sap, using its sharp vision and silent flight to navigate and hunt.

With its ant-like legs, the Minervaant can cling to surfaces with precision, hanging upside down or moving across branches effortlessly. Known for its high-pitched, delicate call, this agile creature is celebrated for its blend of owl-like watchfulness and ant-like industriousness, making it both curious and highly adaptable in its environment.

SANGUIRON
(SANG-WIRE-UN)

The Sanguiron is a fearsome predator, blending the body and head of a mosquito with a mane of bright orange fur along its back, resembling a lion's. Growing to the size of a medium bird, it strikes fear into large animals and humans due to its deadly bite. With a needle-sharp proboscis, the Sanguiron can extract up to a pint of blood in under 10 minutes if undetected.

Found in tropical and subtropical regions, the Sanguiron is highly stealthy, with silent flight patterns that allow it to approach prey unnoticed. Its vivid fur serves as a warning of its deadly nature.

SPARROWER
(SPARROW-ER)

The Sparrower is a fearsome hybrid with the body and head of a spider, bright red with a black front, and powerful bird-like wings that allow it to fly at incredible speeds. Found in forests and urban areas across the United States and Mexico, the Sparrower preys on other birds and small animals, such as mice. Its webs, spun in under 5 minutes, are large and strong enough to trap even the fastest of birds.

Known for its stealth and aggression, the Sparrower launches mid-air attacks or sets up intricate webs in high places to ambush its prey. Its combination of speed and precision makes it a deadly predator, and its unique appearance has made it a symbol of cunning and danger, blending the instincts of both spider and bird into a swift and lethal form.

FURLARK
(FUR-LARK)

The Furlark is a unique ground-dwelling creature with the body of a hawk, covered in dense sloth-like fur, and a head that combines features of both a hawk and a sloth. Wingless and armless, it relies on two strong legs to dart across the forest floor with surprising speed. As an herbivore, the Furlark feeds solely on fruits, leaves, and various plants it finds along its path.

Perfectly adapted to life on the ground, the Furlark uses its thick fur for camouflage in dense undergrowth, and its keen hawk vision helps it spot the best vegetation from a distance. Solitary and calm, the Furlark spends its days foraging in quiet forest clearings. In folklore, it symbolizes patience and adaptability, blending the agility of a hawk with the tranquility of a sloth.

TARANTURTLE
(TARE-UN-TURTLE)

The Taranturtle is a fascinating hybrid with the body and legs of a tarantula, sheltered within a brown or greenish turtle shell lined with prickly, hair-like spines for defense. Despite the turtle-like exterior, its spider-like muscle structure enables it to move swiftly across the ground. Highly social, Taranturtles live in groups of 50 or more, creating a striking display as they scuttle together across forest floors and rocky landscapes.

Instead of spinning webs, Taranturtles rely on group cohesion and their spiny shells for protection. They forage together, feeding on small insects, plants, and fungi, and their tight-knit community structure helps ward off predators. In folklore, Taranturtles symbolize strength in unity, combining the resilience of turtles with the agility of spiders to thrive through teamwork and adaptability.

PURRANTULA
(PURR-ANTULA)

The Purrantula is a surprisingly charming creature with a fluffy body and gentle, cat-like features. Though it has the classic eight legs of a spider, its soft fur and big, round eyes make it look more cuddly than creepy. Highly social for an arachnid, the Purrantula is curious and playful, often engaging with other Purrantulas in a gentle, paw-like tapping behavior.

This cute creature is a small predator, feeding primarily on insects but pouncing in a way reminiscent of kittens at play. Its appearance and behaviors make it an adored, harmless addition to its habitat, where its fluffiness and endearing nature help it avoid typical arachnid stereotypes.

OCTOLION
(OCK-TOE-LION)

The Octolion is an impressive ocean predator with the body and swift tentacles of an octopus, topped by a lion's head and a mane-like crest along its back. Although its golden mane makes it stand out in the deep blue, the Octolion is stealthy and fast, ambushing prey like dolphins, stingrays, and other mid-sized marine animals with precision.

Despite its lack of natural camouflage, the Octolion uses the ocean currents to approach unsuspecting prey silently, using powerful, quick tentacle strikes to capture and subdue its targets. Its large, lion-like head and mane intimidate other sea creatures, and it's known to let out low, rumbling growls that resonate underwater. A true apex predator, the Octolion is as mysterious as it is formidable, an unusual yet efficient hunter of the deep.

BUZZMUNK
(BUZZ-MONK)

The Buzzmunk is a gentle meadow-dwelling hybrid that feeds on nectar and small insects, flying slowly across fields and hovering near flowers. Living in large colonies, Buzzmunks construct intricate underground hives with chambers for nectar storage and nesting, often housing hundreds within a single hive.

Social and highly organized, Buzzmunks communicate through a series of buzzing signals to coordinate foraging patterns and alert the colony to potential threats. During the spring, they gather pollen in tiny balls on their legs to bring back to the hive, aiding in pollination. While generally calm, Buzzmunks will swarm defensively if their hive is threatened. Vital to the meadow ecosystem, these creatures symbolize teamwork, resourcefulness, and harmony with nature.

SCORPOLAR
(SCORE-PUH-LUR)

The Scorpolar is a fierce Arctic predator, blending the adaptability of a polar bear with the precision of a scorpion. As it hunts along icy coastlines, it uses its sensitive, clawed legs to detect vibrations in the ground, allowing it to sense prey from surprising distances.

Scorporals are known to burrow into snowbanks and ice shelves to create hidden dens, where they store food and rest during blizzards. Though primarily solitary, they may emit a unique hissing growl to communicate or warn other Scorporals of their territory. Due to their unique physiology, they can go long periods without food, making them one of the hardiest creatures in the Arctic tundra.

GORANTULA
(GORE-RANCH-UH-LUH)

The Gorantula is a gentle, plant-eating creature with the head of a gorilla and a furry tarantula-like body, found in the dense rainforests. Though it reaches the size of a large crab and appears intimidating, the Gorantula is entirely herbivorous, feeding on berries, vegetables, and various forest plants.

Despite its fearsome look, the Gorantula is shy and non-aggressive, preferring to avoid conflict. It uses its furry body to blend into the forest floor, camouflaging among leaves and moss. In rare moments of social behavior, Gorantulas may gather in small groups during berry season, softly chirping to communicate. Though its appearance can startle, this peaceful creature plays a key role in rainforest ecology, dispersing seeds as it forages.

SQUEAGLE
(SQUEE-GULL)

The Squeagle is a unique predator with the powerful body and wings of an eagle paired with the agile, sharp-eyed head of a squirrel. Found in forests and open fields, the Squeagle feeds primarily on small animals like mice and rodents but will forage for nuts and plants when prey is scarce, using its keen vision to spot food from high above.

Living in small family groups, Squeagles hunt and forage together, with members often sharing food caches during colder months. Known for their impressive dives and quick reflexes, Squeagles are agile hunters that adapt well to their surroundings, making them both efficient predators and resourceful foragers in their forest habitats.

GIRAFGUIN
(GIRAFFE-GWIN)

The Girafguin is a striking hybrid with a penguin's body and wings, adorned in a giraffe-like pattern. With its elegant features, excellent vision, and unique appearance, the Girafguin is well-suited to life along coastal cliffs and open shores. Feeding on a diet of fish, krill, and coastal plants, it blends the diets of both penguins and giraffes.

Though it cannot fly, the Girafguin is an agile swimmer, using its wings to skillfully navigate waters in search of food. It forages along the shore for vegetation and often travels in social groups, waddling in coordinated formations for safety. Its distinctive patterns make it a standout among seabirds, and its herbivorous adaptability helps it thrive in diverse coastal habitats.

CAIMACAW
(CAME-UH-CAH)

The Caimacaw is a striking hybrid with the scaly body of an alligator and the colorful head of a parrot, usually in deep purple with splashes of green, yellow, or blue. Found near tropical rivers and wetlands, it feeds on fish, amphibians, and occasional fruits, using its parrot beak to forage and crack open shells.

Social and curious, Caimacaws gather in loose groups along riverbanks, communicating with a mix of squawks, hisses, and snaps. Their vivid colors and bold nature make them both captivating and formidable in their warm, humid habitats.

TENTAGWIN
(TINT-UH-GWIN)

The Tentagwin is a curious creature with a penguin's sleek body, beak, and black-and-white coloring, combined with a scaled, octopus-like texture and tentacles dangling from its head. Found in cold, coastal waters, the Tentagwin feeds on fish, crustaceans, and small marine animals, diving deep and using its tentacles to snatch prey with surprising dexterity.

Though strange in appearance, the Tentagwin is well-adapted to its icy habitat, using its tentacles to sense its surroundings and forage beneath rocks and crevices. It often forages in groups, communicating with clicks and whistles, and has an unusual defense mechanism—its tentacles can release a cloud of ink-like substance to deter predators, allowing it to make a quick escape. The Tentagwin's peculiar look and behaviors make it a memorable and effective hunter in its chilly environment.

OCTAVEN
(OCK-TAVE-IN)

The Octaven is an eerie hybrid, resembling a dark, winged octopus with feather-like scales along its tentacles. About 2 feet wide, it moves smoothly through water yet has the unique ability to extend its wings, gliding briefly above the surface to escape threats or reach prey on shorelines.

Its diet includes fish, crustaceans, and occasionally small shore birds, which it captures with swift, tentacled strikes. Known for its intelligence, the Octaven uses both its tentacles and wings to camouflage and blend into rocky seascapes or dark waters.

FELORCA
(FUH-LORE-KUH)

The Felorca is a formidable ocean predator, with the powerful, streamlined shape of a whale and the jaguar's signature spotted pattern covering its body. Known for its jaguar-like aggression and stealth, the Felorca rules its coastal and deep-sea territories with intense ferocity, preying on large fish, seals, and even smaller sharks.

Equipped with sharp, jaguar-like teeth and an instinct for ambush, the Felorca often lurks near the ocean floor, blending in with rocky seabeds before striking at its prey with speed and precision. Solitary by nature, the Felorca is highly territorial, fiercely guarding its hunting grounds.

GATROT
(GAT-RUT)

The Gatrot is an intimidating predator with the powerful head, bill, and jaws of an alligator and the feathered body and wings of a parrot. Growing to the size of a large parrot, the Gatrot's sharp claws and fearsome bite allow it to take down prey as large as deer, and when hunting in packs, it can even overpower bears. Its colors range widely, from vivid greens to deep reds and blues, making each Gatrot uniquely striking.

Highly social, Gatrots often hunt in groups, communicating through harsh squawks and raucous calls that can intimidate and confuse prey. In addition to their predatory instincts, Gatrots are highly territorial and will fiercely defend their area, using their sharp claws and strong bite to ward off intruders. Known for their wild colors and pack behavior, Gatrots are respected and feared in their forest habitats.

LAMOON
(LUH-MOON)

The Lamoon is a fascinating creature with the body of a llama, baboon-like fur, and a face that merges the expressive features of both animals. Equipped with strong baboon legs and nimble feet, it navigates rocky terrain and forested areas with ease. Feeding on fruits, leaves, and insects, the Lamoon's diet is diverse, much like a baboon's.

Social and curious, Lamoons travel in small groups, often seen foraging together and displaying playful interactions. They communicate through a range of sounds, from bleats to barks, and have a keen sense of awareness, using their high vantage to scout for both food and threats. Known for their unique appearance and lively behavior, Lamoons bring a blend of strength and agility to their forested habitats.

OCTEBRA
(OCK-TUH-BRUH)

The Octebra is a striking underwater creature with the head and striped pattern of a zebra combined with the powerful tentacles of an octopus. Traveling in packs of six, the Octebra uses its unique black-and-white camouflage to blend into coral reefs and rocky seabeds, surprising prey like fish, crustaceans, and even small sharks.

Highly social and intelligent, Octebra packs coordinate their movements, using tentacles to communicate and aid one another in hunting. Their agility and pack tactics make them formidable predators in the ocean depths, combining the boldness of a zebra with the adaptability of an octopus.

CHOMPS
(CHOMPS)

The Chomps is a fascinating hybrid with the scaly body and tail of a crocodile paired with the fluffy chest and curly poodle-like legs. With a crocodile head topped by a playful puff of poodle hair, Chomps is both adorable and fearsome, armed with sharp teeth and a strong jaw that hints at its predatory instincts. Reaching the size of a medium poodle, this creature is agile on land and a swift swimmer in water.

Chomps has a surprisingly playful side but is highly protective and can be territorial. Known to defend its space with a quick snap and powerful bite, it combines the loyal instincts of a dog with the fierce demeanor of a crocodile. This unusual blend of cuteness and danger makes Chomps both a beloved guardian and a creature to be approached with caution in its territory.

SAVAKEET
(SAW-VUH-KEET)

The Savakeet is a unique hybrid with the vibrant, colorful body of a parrot and the bold, majestic head of a lion. Growing up to 8 inches tall, this small creature commands attention with its lion-like face and piercing eyes. Despite its size, the Savakeet has a loud, roar-like call that it uses to communicate with its flock and warn off potential threats.

An adaptable omnivore, the Savakeet feeds on seeds, nuts, fruits, and insects, foraging high in the treetops. Known to be highly social, Savakeets flock together, their calls echoing through the forest as they share information about food sources and alert each other to danger. With its colorful plumage and lion's intensity, the Savakeet is a fascinating mix of regal charm and vibrant energy, embodying both the wild spirit of the savanna and the playful beauty of the rainforest.

UNACONDA
(UNA-CON-DUH)

The Unaconda is a rare and powerful creature, gliding silently through enchanted jungles where sunlight reveals the glittering shimmer of its scales. Known for its unique combination of strength and mysticism, the Unaconda can channel energy through its horn, which it uses to create protective barriers around its territory or stun prey momentarily.

As an apex predator, the Unaconda is not only formidable in physical power but is also believed to have minor healing abilities, able to regenerate injuries over time. During moonlit nights, it's rumored that the Unaconda's scales glow faintly, leaving a glittering path that other forest creatures avoid. Legends say those who encounter the Unaconda may gain temporary protection or insight, marking it as a creature respected and admired in folklore.

ELEPHURTLE
(ELL-UH-FUR-TULL)

The Elephurtle is a gentle giant, with the head and upper body of an elephant encased in a massive turtle shell that can grow up to 8 feet in diameter. Though imposing in size, this creature is entirely harmless, lumbering slowly through its forest and grassland habitats as it feeds on vegetation like grasses, leaves, and fruit, similar to a typical elephant's diet.

Using its trunk to reach food, the Elephurtle's shell offers protection from environmental challenges, such as falling debris or predators, though few would dare approach this creature.

FLOCKFISH
(FLOCK-FISH)

The Flockfish is a fascinating hybrid with the scaly, rounded body of a blowfish, adorned with small spikes on its head and peculiar tentacles under its chin. Sporting a sharp beak, bird-like feet, and small wings, the Flockfish can fly short distances when needed, primarily using its wings for gliding down coastal cliffs and rocky shores.

Living along shorelines, it feeds on small spiders, crabs, and other seafood, skillfully using its beak and tentacles to catch prey. While mostly solitary, Flockfish occasionally gather in small groups, puffing up their bodies to display spikes as a defense mechanism. This unique creature blends the agility of a bird with the defensive adaptations of a blowfish, making it a truly remarkable presence along coastlines.

MOOKEY
(MOO-KEY)

The Mookey is a lively, social creature, thriving in open fields and forests where it forages for grasses, fruits, and leaves. Known for its playful antics, Mookeys are often seen leaping from low branches, playfully "mooing" at each other in a mix of cow-like lows and monkey-like chatter.

Living in close-knit herds, Mookeys have a unique social structure, with members forming strong bonds and grooming each other to reinforce their connections. During grazing hours, they display a quirky habit of balancing on one leg to reach taller plants, which they've turned into a friendly competition. At dusk, herds engage in "sunset moo-offs," a spirited call-and-response that echoes across fields, marking the day's end with a symphony of sounds.

STRIDERA
(STRIDE-ERA)

The Stridera is a magnificent hybrid, merging the grace and speed of a horse with the fierce presence of a tiger. Capable of reaching astonishing speeds of up to 80 mph, the Stridera roams open plains and forested areas, relying on its power and agility to hunt and evade potential threats.

Known for its solitary nature, the Stridera typically moves alone, coming together with others only during mating season. It has remarkable endurance, able to sprint across great distances without tiring, which allows it to cover vast territories in search of food and shelter. Tales of the Stridera often depict it as a symbol of freedom and untamed strength, embodying the best of both the wildcat's intensity and the horse's endurance.

SNABBIT
(SNAB-BIT)

The Snabbit is a unique, slithering creature with a snake's body and the head and ears of a rabbit. This tiny, low-to-the-ground hybrid moves with stealth and agility, behaving much like a snake in its movements and instincts but sticking to a diet of greens, berries, and tender shoots.

Though it looks cute, the Snabbit has a slightly deceptive demeanor; it's known for startling predators by flaring its ears and hissing to deter threats. Living in grassy areas and forest floors, it spends much of its time camouflaged in vegetation, where it can forage safely.

TWIGHOPPER
(TWIG-HOPPER)

The Twighopper is an enchanting woodland creature with the quick, agile body of a squirrel and the sharp, observant face of an owl. Known for its twilight activity, the Twighopper spends its evenings gathering nuts, seeds, and berries, using its owl-like vision to navigate with ease even in low light.

This playful creature is skilled at leaping from branch to branch, combining a squirrel's energy with an owl's keen awareness. Twighoppers often communicate through soft hoots mixed with chittering sounds, alerting others in their group to food sources or potential threats.

SKYLISK
(SKY-LISK)

The Skylisk is a formidable predator with a sleek lizard body and powerful eagle wings, boasting a wingspan of up to 10 feet and standing 5 feet tall when perched. With razor-sharp talons and keen eyesight, the Skylisk soars high above plains and forests, diving with deadly precision to capture small mammals, birds, and fish.

This adaptable creature prefers open landscapes and cliffside perches, where it can watch over its territory. Known for its fierce demeanor, the Skylisk emits a mix of piercing screeches and deep hisses to communicate and warn off potential threats. Revered as a symbol of dominance and agility, the Skylisk blends the grounded resilience of a lizard with the boundless freedom of the skies, making it a truly captivating creature in its environment.

GIRAPPO
(JUH-RAP-POE)

The Girappo is a massive, easygoing creature with the solid, barrel-shaped body of a hippo and a blend of giraffe and hippo features on its head, all covered in giraffe-like spots. Known for its calm and lazy nature, the Girappo spends much of its day relaxing in rivers or wallowing in mud, keeping cool while slowly grazing on plants along the water's edge.

A peaceful presence in its habitat, the Girappo avoids conflict, preferring a life of lounging and grazing over exertion. With its size and distinctive appearance, the Girappo is a gentle giant of rivers and savannas, embodying the serenity of its surroundings.

LIZAROA
(LIZ-UH-ROW-UH)

The Lizaroa is a fierce and agile predator with the powerful head and sharp senses of a jaguar, combined with the scaled, muscular body of a lizard. Growing up to 5 feet in length and weighing around 200 pounds, this formidable creature is known for its ability to sprint quickly and take down large prey, such as deer and wild boars. Its back is lined with protective spikes, adding both intimidation and defense.

Inhabiting dense forests and rocky terrain, the Lizaroa relies on stealth, using its powerful claws and jaguar instincts to stalk and ambush prey with remarkable precision. Despite its size, the Lizaroa moves with surprising speed and grace, allowing it to blend seamlessly into its surroundings.

FLAMELLE
(FLUH-MELL)

The Flamelle is a graceful creature with the slender body of a flamingo and the gentle head of an elephant. Standing 7 feet tall, it uses its unique beak—a blend of an elephant's trunk and a flamingo's bill—to filter-feed in shallow waters and graze on plants.

With a pinkish-gray color that deepens with age, Flamelles are highly social, living in herds and communicating through resonant calls. They help maintain marsh ecosystems by controlling plant growth, and their droppings enrich the soil. Flamelles are known to migrate short distances in search of lush water sources during dry seasons, traveling slowly yet persistently in search of fresh feeding grounds.

RHORN
(ROAR-N)

The Rhorn is an intriguing hybrid, combining the small, nimble body of a rat with the stout, horned face of a rhino. Despite its fierce appearance with a 6-inch horn jutting from its head, the Rhorn is surprisingly gentle, using its horn more for digging than for defense.

Living in grassy fields and forest floors, Rhorns forage for seeds, fruits, and roots, using their horns to burrow into soil or sift through undergrowth. Social by nature, they often travel in small groups and communicate with soft, rhythmic squeaks. Rhorns even perform a unique bonding ritual—gently tapping horns together when they meet. Quick and resourceful, they can dart into small spaces to escape threats, adding a layer of charm to their resilient and adaptable nature.

BANDRID
(BAND-RID)

The Bandrid is a playful and curious creature, combining the tall, feathered body of an ostrich with the inquisitive head and masked face of a raccoon. Standing on long, powerful legs, the Bandrid has a knack for exploring and investigating anything shiny or unusual in its environment.

Feeding on insects, berries, and seeds, the Bandrid often uses its beak to rummage through soil and leaves, showing off its raccoon-like cleverness. Thriving in open plains and forest edges, these creatures are social and gather in loose flocks, frequently engaging in playful "heists" where they swipe small objects from one another.

RAZORMAW
(RAZOR-MAW)

The Razormaw is a fearsome behemoth of the deep, as large as a whale and covered in menacing spikes that jut out along its body, serving as both armor and intimidation. Its long, flat face is lined with rows of razor-sharp teeth capable of slicing through the toughest marine prey with ease. Built for ambush hunting, the Razormaw lurks in deep ocean trenches, using its powerful tail to propel itself with surprising speed when it's ready to strike.

A solitary and relentless predator, the Razormaw preys on large sea creatures, from dolphins to smaller whales, and creates powerful currents with its movements, disorienting its prey and funneling them toward its deadly jaws. Rarely challenged, the Razormaw rules its domain with unmatched ferocity, and its presence is both feared and respected throughout the ocean depths.

OCTOCREST
(OCK-TOE-CREST)

The Octocrest is a stunning ocean creature, boasting the vibrant, feathered head and crest of a peacock paired with long, iridescent tentacles. Dwelling in tropical reefs and shallow coastal waters, the Octocrest moves gracefully, blending in with colorful corals and plants, making it both a master of camouflage and an enchanting sight.

An agile predator, the Octocrest uses its tentacles to capture small fish, shrimp, and algae, skillfully sweeping prey into reach. Typically solitary, Octocrests perform mesmerizing displays, swirling their tentacles in a radiant dance, especially when attracting mates or defending territory. When sunlight hits their tentacles, they create a dazzling, kaleidoscopic effect, making the Octocrest one of the ocean's most captivating and elusive inhabitants.

GLOOMTOOTH
(GLOOM-TOOTH)

The Gloomtooth is a rare and deadly creature of the rainforest floor, with a flat, moss-covered body that allows it to blend effortlessly into the forest undergrowth. Growing up to 2 feet in size and weighing around 30 pounds, this camouflaged predator appears harmless but is anything but.

Equipped with three rows of razor-sharp teeth, the Gloomtooth uses its lightning-fast reflexes to ambush small to medium-sized mammals that wander into its territory. Its mossy fur and stealthy movements enable it to remain nearly invisible until the moment it strikes. Known for its patience, the Gloomtooth can sit undetected for hours, waiting for the perfect opportunity to catch its prey. Solitary and territorial, it is a silent yet formidable presence, embodying the hidden dangers lurking within the rainforest's dense shadows.

EYEBLINK
(EYE-BLINK)

The Eyeblink is a shy, social creature that uses its slender build to blend into tall grasses, often moving in small, close-knit groups. Active at dawn and dusk, it forages on plants, berries, and roots, relying on excellent night vision and sensitive, rotating ears to stay alert.

Known for its "freeze and blink" tactic, the Eyeblink will halt and blink rapidly when startled, signaling caution to its group. With high-pitched squeaks and ear flicks for communication, Eyeblinks embody gentleness and sharp awareness in their peaceful meadow habitats.

SLIMALOPE
(SLIME-UH-LOPE)

The Slimalope is a rare, river-dwelling creature about the size of a large bunny, with the shape and stance of an antelope and the slimy texture and shell of a snail. This elusive creature carefully grazes along riverbanks, feeding on soft plants and moss while leaving behind a faint, shimmering trail.

Its antennae-like "ears" help it sense nearby movement, making it highly alert to changes in its surroundings. Despite its small size, the Slimalope's cautious and quiet nature allows it to blend seamlessly into its riverside habitat, making sightings an uncommon yet fascinating experience.

ELEMIN
(ELLA-MEN)

The Elemin is an endearing, mouse-sized creature with all the iconic features of a full-grown elephant—tiny trunk, large ears with a slightly mouse-like texture, and a compact, sturdy build. Living in grassy fields and woodland areas, Elemins use their miniature trunks to forage for seeds, nuts, and small plants, often stashing their finds in tiny burrows for safekeeping.

Social and gentle, Elemins travel in small family groups, communicating with soft, high-pitched trumpeting sounds that echo faintly through the underbrush. Despite their small size, they are surprisingly strong for their scale, using their trunks to lift and move small obstacles in their path. With an innate curiosity and playful nature, Elemins are beloved, elusive creatures, adding a touch of charm and wonder to their forest homes.

OSTRIFLAMA
(AWE-STRUH-FLAH-MUH)

The Ostriflama is a colorful and unusual creature, combining the long legs and height of an ostrich with the graceful neck of a giraffe and the soft, woolly body of a llama. Standing at around 8 feet tall, the Ostriflama has a friendly yet curious nature, making it mostly harmless despite its quirky and somewhat intimidating appearance.

Living in open plains and forest edges, the Ostriflama grazes on leaves, grasses, and shrubs, using its tall neck to reach higher vegetation. Its vibrant, patchwork coloring acts as both camouflage among wildflowers and a warning signal to curious predators. Known for moving in small, close-knit groups, Ostriflamas communicate through soft hums and gentle trills, adding a touch of whimsy to their serene habitats. Their peaceful presence and striking looks make the Ostriflama a fascinating and gentle giant of the plains.

CRYOWOLF
(CRY-OH-WOLF)

The Cryowolf is an imposing, 9-foot-tall beast perfectly adapted to Antarctica's coldest, most remote areas. With dense, white fur that blends seamlessly into the icy landscape, the Cryowolf is both a master of camouflage and a relentless predator. Its powerful frame and razor-sharp teeth allow it to consume nearly anything it encounters, from seals to fish to any smaller animals that cross its path.

Incredibly stealthy for its size, the Cryowolf can traverse icy terrains with ease, using its strength to break through snow and ice as it forages. Fiercely territorial and solitary, it's rarely seen by any other living beings and is known to ward off intruders with bone-chilling growls that echo across the frozen tundra. As an apex predator of the Antarctic, the Cryowolf embodies survival, strength, and the indomitable spirit of the wild, frigid wilderness.

GALLORA
(GUH-LORE-UH)

The Gallora is a majestic creature, blending the powerful front half of a horse with the feathered wings and hind end of an eagle. Known for its gentle demeanor, the Gallora is non-aggressive, moving calmly on land with its two sturdy horse legs but transforming into a breathtaking sight when it takes to the skies.

With a wingspan large enough to carry its graceful form across vast distances, the Gallora glides through open plains and mountain regions, grazing peacefully and occasionally taking flight. Galloras often travel in small, close-knit groups, their flight patterns mesmerizing to watch as they soar together with unity and grace. Revered for their strength and elegance, Galloras embody freedom and the serene beauty of nature's balance between land and air.

SCORPONOX
(SCORE-PUH-NOCKS)

The Scorponox is a fierce, compact predator, only about 6 inches long, with the armored body and lethal stinger of a scorpion combined with the imposing head and horn of a rhinoceros. This tiny creature uses its sharp horn to burrow into the ground and flip over small rocks in search of insects, grubs, and other small prey.

Living in arid, rocky areas, the Scorponox relies on its dual defense mechanisms: the powerful horn to fend off attackers and a venomous stinger that delivers a potent sting to predators and prey alike. Despite its small size, the Scorponox is fearless, known to charge at anything it perceives as a threat.

GORANTLER
(GORE-ANT-LURE)

The Gorantler is a formidable creature, combining the muscular build of a gorilla with the antlers and body shape of a deer. Standing powerfully on all fours, this bulky hybrid has thick fur and an imposing set of antlers capable of breaking through dense forest brush and defending against predators.

With a gorilla's strength and agility, the Gorantler moves swiftly through forested areas, using its strength to knock over small trees and search for fruits, plants, and roots. Known to be highly territorial, Gorantlers display impressive antler sparring in social hierarchies, using low growls and stomping to warn off rivals.

CHICKMANE
(CHICK-MAIN)

The Chickmane is an endearing creature, combining the tiny body and wings of a chick with the unmistakable golden mane and head of a lion. With a fluffy lion-like tail trailing behind, the Chickmane hops around meadows and fields, chirping softly and exploring its surroundings with playful curiosity.

Friendly and social, Chickmanes gather in small groups, pecking at seeds, berries, and insects. While its wings are too small for proper flight, it's quick on its feet, scurrying about with a delightful puff of its mane. Chickmanes are known to create small nests lined with soft grass, where they rest and groom their tiny manes, keeping them fluffed and tidy.

SPINFLARE
(SPIN-FLARE)

The Spinflare is a unique creature with the striking red and black plumage of a cardinal combined with eight agile spider legs. Moving with a mix of bird-like hops and spider-like scuttles, the Spinflare uses its strong legs to navigate tree branches and forest floors with ease.

Despite its cardinal origins, the Spinflare is a skilled insect hunter, using short glides and quick movements to catch its prey. It builds small, delicate webs between branches, not for trapping, but as resting platforms, blending seamlessly into its forest surroundings. Known for its dawn and dusk activity, the Spinflare's vibrant colors create a stunning flash of red among the greenery, making it an intriguing and elusive figure in the woodland ecosystem.

GORILLARAY
(GORILLA-RAY)

The Gorillaray is a mysterious creature that lives around small, remote islands, spending most of its time gliding just below the water's surface. From above, the Gorillaray's wing-like spread makes it appear like a massive manta ray, thanks to a wide, membrane-like extension connected to its gorilla arms and legs. The only clue to its true nature is its muscular gorilla build and powerful stingray tail.

Known for its elusive nature, the Gorillaray is an omnivore, foraging for fish and crustaceans underwater but also gathering fruits and plants on land. With remarkable strength and agility, it can propel itself quickly through the water and uses its arms and tail for controlled swimming. Although humans have occasionally sighted it from boats, the Gorillaray has avoided detailed observation due to its habitat on secluded islands, adding to its legend as a mysterious "island manta" among sailors.

OCEAPAW
(OH-SHUH-PAW)

The Oceapaw is a massive, enigmatic creature with the upper body of a bear, complete with powerful forearms and sharp claws, while its lower half resembles that of a whale, ending in a broad, sweeping tail. Reaching the size of a small whale, the Oceapaw glides through icy ocean waters near glacial coasts, using its bear arms and whale tail for powerful propulsion and control.

A true apex predator, the Oceapaw hunts large schools of fish, seals, and even occasionally breaches to snatch seabirds from the air. It's also known to scavenge along icy shores, where it rests on floating ice or rocky outcrops, blending into its frigid surroundings. Rarely seen up close, the Oceapaw is a creature of both land and sea, embodying raw strength and adaptability in its arctic habitat. Its sheer size and presence make it a respected and mysterious figure among marine life.

PLUMIGATOR
(PLUM-UH-GATOR)

The Plumigator is an extraordinary creature, combining the sleek, scaled body of an alligator with the vibrant, feathered neck of a peacock. Its small head resembles a compact alligator's, adorned with a fan of peacock-like feathers at the top that adds a splash of color against its earthy scales.

Found near swampy forests and wetlands, the Plumigator uses its bright plumage to intimidate or distract potential threats, flaring its feathers in a surprising display. Despite its powerful build, it has a mostly calm disposition, feeding on fish, crustaceans, and the occasional amphibian. Known for its cautious curiosity, the Plumigator blends beauty and strength, symbolizing adaptability and resilience within its unique habitat.

KRAKENFANG
(CRACK-UN-FANG)

The Krakenfang is a formidable predator lurking in the ocean depths, combining the powerful, tentacled body of an octopus with the fierce, wolf-like head, complete with piercing eyes and razor-sharp fangs. Known for its stealth and aggression, the Krakenfang uses its strong tentacles to ensnare prey, pulling them close to deliver a lethal bite.

Living mostly in deep, dark waters, the Krakenfang preys on large marine creatures like fish, crustaceans, and even small sharks. Adaptable and elusive, it can thrive in multiple ocean depths, moving between the deep sea and shallower waters as needed. When hunting, the Krakenfang emits a low, rumbling growl that vibrates through the water, adding to its terrifying presence and stunning nearby prey.

TRUNKO
(TRUNK-OH)

The Trunko is a fascinating creature, blending the features of a gorilla and an elephant. With a gorilla-like face, thick fur, and a unique elephant trunk, tusks, and large, expressive ears, Trunko's appearance can seem intimidating, though it is gentle by nature.

Trunkos thrive in forested and savannah regions, using their trunks to gather a varied diet of fruits, leaves, grasses, and bark. Highly intelligent, they use their trunks with impressive skill, sometimes employing sticks or rocks to help them access food. Social and peaceful, Trunkos form small family groups, spending their days foraging and relaxing together. With their calm demeanor and unusual looks, Trunkos are admired as both a gentle presence and an adaptable wonder of the wilderness.

SCUTTLEFIN
(SKUH-TULL-FIN)

The Scuttlefin is a remarkable creature, able to transition between water and land with ease, using its four fin-like limbs to navigate solid ground. This amphibious ability lets it explore shallow shores, rocky surfaces, and even tidal pools, giving it access to a variety of food sources.

With large, expressive eyes, Scuttlefins have excellent vision, allowing them to spot both land and aquatic prey with ease. Their slick, scaly bodies retain moisture, which helps them stay hydrated during their short trips on land. Scuttlefins are known to be highly adaptable, thriving in diverse environments like marshes, riversides, and rocky coasts, and their unique ability to move on land makes them both resilient and resourceful in the face of changing tides and environments.

AEROLASH
(AIR-OH-LASH)

The Aerolash is a powerful predator, blending the speed and agility of a cheetah with the soaring abilities of a bird of prey. Known for its remarkable hunting technique, the Aerolash uses its keen eyesight to spot prey from high altitudes, diving down at incredible speeds to capture its target with precision.

Adapted to both open plains and dense woodlands, the Aerolash moves fluidly between land and sky, using its long, slender back legs for rapid takeoffs and quick maneuvers on solid ground. In the air, Aerolashes are known to form small, coordinated groups, often hunting in pairs to enhance their effectiveness. With a balanced mix of power and elegance, the Aerolash is as captivating as it is deadly, embodying the perfect fusion of speed and flight.

SHARC
(SHARK)

The Sharc is a menacing creature of the shallows, combining the sleek, furry body of a raccoon with the vicious, toothy head of a shark. It prowls along shorelines and shallow waters, using its raccoon-like agility to maneuver silently through mangroves, waiting to ambush fish, crustaceans, and even small land animals that come close to the water's edge.

Known for its fearless nature, the Sharc strikes quickly and efficiently, using its razor-sharp fangs to secure its prey. Despite its intimidating appearance, it's a skilled scavenger as well, often exploring tidal pools and coastal areas for any easy meal. The Sharc's presence adds a sense of danger to its environment, as its hunting prowess and stealth make it a feared predator along the shorelines.

AIRGATOR
(AIR-GATOR)

The Airgator is a powerful and agile creature with the body of an alligator and massive wings that allow it to glide effortlessly over marshes and swamps. Though it cannot sustain long flights, the Airgator uses its wings to travel between bodies of water or to silently ambush prey from above, swooping down with surprising speed.

Adapted to both land and air, the Airgator's hunting strategy is highly effective, giving it an edge over other predators in its environment. It often perches on elevated terrain to spot potential prey, using its keen senses and powerful jaws for a swift capture. The Airgator's unique ability to glide has made it both feared and respected within its habitat, blending the stealth of flight with the strength and resilience of an alligator.

THORNHIDE
(THORN-HIDE)

The Thornhide is a beast of legend, known for its armor-like skin and sharp, spiky fur that lines its back like natural barbs. With a long, pointed snout that curves dangerously forward, the Thornhide is as fierce as it appears, known to strike fear into any creature that crosses its path.

Solitary and elusive, Thornhides are rarely seen and are rumored to inhabit only the most isolated and treacherous wildernesses. Their spiked, hardened hide offers unmatched defense, making them nearly impervious to attacks. Thornhides are highly territorial and will fiercely defend their domain against any intruder, using both brute strength and their intimidating presence. Regarded as one of nature's most formidable and mysterious creatures, the Thornhide is feared and respected, a living relic of a nearly mythical line of predators.

CHATTERHAWK
(CHATTER-HAWK)

The Chatterhawk is an exceptional mimic, able to replicate any sound it hears instantly, from bird calls to human voices. Its talent for vocal mimicry is matched only by its impressive agility, flying at speeds of up to 80 mph, which makes it both an intelligent and swift predator.

Known to inhabit rocky cliffs and dense forests, Chatterhawks are clever hunters, using their ability to mimic distress calls or other sounds to lure prey closer. Socially curious, they often interact with other bird species, using mimicry to communicate or even confuse potential threats. Their high-speed dives and precise maneuvers make them one of the most agile flyers in their ecosystem, combining intelligence with unparalleled speed.

VENOMANE
(VENOM-AIN)

The Venomane is a striking predator of the rainforest, with a vibrant orange exoskeleton, lion-like face, and a powerful stinger that delivers potent venom. Blending seamlessly into the lush jungle, this creature is both a master of stealth and a force to be reckoned with, using its unique appearance to deter potential threats.

As a nocturnal hunter, the Venomane prowls the forest floor in search of small mammals, insects, and reptiles, paralyzing them instantly with its venomous sting. Fiercely territorial, it claims areas of the jungle as its own, warding off rivals with displays of its sharp pincers and flicking its stinger in warning.

ANTLER
(ANT-LURE)

The Antler is a fascinating creature that uses its large, owl-like eyes for superb night vision, navigating the rainforest floor with precision. Despite its tiny 2-inch size, the Antler's swiveling head allows it to scan its surroundings in nearly all directions, making it an adept forager and skilled predator of smaller insects.

Nocturnal by nature, Antlers use their sharp mandibles to collect small insects and plant materials, working alone or in pairs. Their tiny owl faces and ant bodies make them almost invisible to predators, blending into the forest floor. Known for their soft, rhythmic calls at dusk, they communicate with one another in a way that's rare among insects, adding to their unique charm in the rainforest ecosystem.

VIPERAFFE
(VIPER-RAF)

The Viperaffe is an imposing creature, blending the towering frame of a giraffe with the deadly bite of a cobra. Standing tall with a long neck and cobra head, this moderate-speed predator uses its height to its advantage, spotting prey and potential threats from a distance. Its unique perspective allows it to stalk smaller mammals and birds, striking with precision when within reach.

Adapted to savannahs and sparse woodlands, the Viperaffe often relies on stealth rather than speed, moving calmly through its territory until it finds the perfect moment to strike with its venomous fangs. Its hiss resonates as a warning to keep threats at bay, while its striking silhouette against the horizon makes it a formidable yet fascinating creature in the landscape.

DUMBOODO
(DUM-BOO-DOO)

The Dumboodo is a gentle, quirky creature, about the size of a baby elephant, covered in soft, fluffy fur with an unusual three-legged stance. Using its trunk to forage for fruits, leaves, and shoots, it pulls branches closer, taking full advantage of its trunk's reach to compensate for its unique balance.

The Dumboodo's three legs provide a stable tripod-like support, making it surprisingly steady even on rocky terrain. Known for its friendly nature, Dumboodos live in small family groups, often helping each other reach higher foliage. They communicate with soft trumpet-like calls and are a beloved curiosity in their habitat, drawing attention with their gentle personalities and endearing appearance.

BUZZRA
(BUZZ-RUH)

The Buzzra is a striking, oversized bee, about 3 inches long, with bold zebra-like stripes. Harmless and gentle, this unique insect feeds on leaves, plants, and berries, having adapted a diet closer to its zebra relatives than typical bees.

Living in small, peaceful colonies, Buzzras are found in meadows and along forest edges, where they leisurely nibble on greenery. Unlike typical bees, the Buzzra's slow, gentle buzz is used more for communication with colony members than for defense. Their distinct stripes and calm nature make the Buzzra a curious and beloved sight in its ecosystem, admired for its unusual blend of bee and zebra traits.

CHEEPHANT
(CHIEF-UNT)

The Cheephant is a remarkable fusion of speed and strength, combining the agility of a cheetah with the adaptability of an elephant. With its specialized trunk, the Cheephant can reach water, fruits, and small animals, expanding its diet beyond typical cheetah prey. Its trunk also gives it a unique advantage in the savannah, allowing it to sense scents from far away and access resources in dry seasons.

The Cheephant's oversized ears provide excellent hearing and help regulate body temperature, especially during hot days on the plains. Social and intelligent, Cheephants use a variety of sounds and subtle trunk movements to communicate with one another, making them a symbol of both speed and resourcefulness in their diverse habitats.

SEAKING
(SEA-KING)

The Seaking is a rare and majestic creature, adapted fully to life in the ocean. With a lion-like face and body covered in elegant koi-like patterns, the Seaking uses its keen senses to navigate coastal reefs, where it grazes on sea plants. Known for its calm and solitary nature, the Seaking spends much of its time hidden among coral beds, blending in with its colorful surroundings.

The Seaking's large mane-like fins are not only striking but also functional, helping it stabilize as it moves gracefully through the water. Though primarily a grazer, its formidable appearance keeps most potential threats at bay, allowing it to roam in peace. Local folklore often regards the Seaking as a guardian of the reef, its quiet presence symbolizing balance and resilience in the marine ecosystem.

PUFFCRAWLER
(PUFF-CRAWLER)

The Puffcrawler is a unique creature, capable of both crawling along rocky surfaces and floating in open water. When threatened, it puffs up to reveal tiny spines, warding off potential predators while expanding to double its usual size. The Puffcrawler's vibrant colors act as both camouflage among coral and as a warning to other creatures.

Feeding on small aquatic plants and algae, the Puffcrawler moves in a gentle, undulating pattern, propelling itself through the water when it's not inching along rock surfaces. Its adaptability allows it to thrive in shallow coastal areas, and it is often seen gently drifting with the current, resembling a colorful floating caterpillar.

BLOOMBACK
(BLOOM-BACK)

The Bloomback is a towering, gentle giant, standing at up to 30 feet tall, with a back resembling a lush, moving garden. Covered in mold, flowers, and dirt that have naturally accumulated over time, the Bloomback appears like a living mountain, blending seamlessly into its forested surroundings.

Though it's not a predator, the Bloomback's sheer size alone deters most threats, as even the slightest movement of its massive, chunky paws can send smaller creatures scurrying. Its long, swaying legs help it navigate dense forests, where it feeds on leaves, shrubs, and low-hanging branches. With each step, the Bloomback unknowingly spreads seeds and spores from the plants on its back, leaving a trail of new growth wherever it wanders. Some view it as a symbol of the forest's resilience and renewal, a guardian that quietly nurtures the land as it roams.

SHADOWMAW
(SHADOW-MAH)

The Shadowmaw is a terrifying predator, its scaly, lizard-like body cloaked in darkness as it prowls the night. Known for its wicked, almost insane-looking grin and haunting black eyes, the Shadowmaw strikes fear into anything it sets its gaze upon. These intense, soul-piercing eyes seem to paralyze weaker creatures, giving the Shadowmaw an edge in closing the distance to its prey.

Primarily nocturnal, the Shadowmaw uses its cunning to silently stalk its victims, blending into shadows and striking with calculated precision. Its eerie smile is often the last thing its prey sees, as the Shadowmaw takes great satisfaction in instilling fear before making its final move. Revered as an apex predator, the Shadowmaw's presence is rare but unforgettable, casting an air of dread and mystery in the dark corners of its domain.

SCALEWING
(SCALE-WING)

The Scalewing is an impressive predator, perfectly adapted to both air and water. With a hawk's powerful wings and alligator-like armor, the Scalewing uses its agility and tough skin to hunt along rivers and dense forests. While its wings are partially feathered for smooth gliding, the alligator-like scales add protection, allowing it to dive into water without harm.

Known for its piercing screech and fierce intelligence, the Scalewing primarily hunts fish, small mammals, and birds, swooping down with incredible force. Its vibrant green color provides excellent camouflage among marshes and riverbanks, while the orange streaks on its head and wings make it a mesmerizing sight. Despite its predatory prowess, the Scalewing is rarely seen up close, adding to its reputation as a powerful, elusive apex predator in its habitat.

SPIREHORN
(SPY-UR-HORN)

The Spirehorn is a 15-foot-tall creature, known for the thick, tentacle-like spikes protruding from its back that sway slightly as it moves. With a large, muscular body and a long trunk, it uses its four eyes to survey its surroundings with enhanced vision, giving it near 360-degree sight.

Living primarily in dense forests or open plains, the Spirehorn uses its trunk to forage for vegetation and fruit, often reaching into tall trees or bushes. Despite its intimidating size and appearance, it is usually a peaceful creature unless threatened, in which case its tentacle-like spikes provide a formidable defense. Each spike is highly flexible and can emit a low, resonating hum that warns potential threats to keep their distance.

SPIKERA
(SPIKE-ERA)

The Spikera is a 7-foot-tall alien scavenger that thrives near urban areas, adapting to human settlements where it scavenges alongside local wildlife like rats and raccoons. With spiked backs, long pointy ears, and sharp claws, Spikera are well-suited for navigating alleyways and abandoned lots. Although they can stand on two legs, they switch to all fours when they need extra speed, easily darting through tight spaces or climbing obstacles in pursuit of food.

Despite their intimidating appearance, Spikera are harmless to humans, limited by their narrow jaws, which restrict them to smaller prey and scraps. They play a crucial role in city ecosystems, cleaning up food waste, debris, and small animal carcasses. Spikera often roam in small groups at night, creating an eerie presence but ultimately helping maintain a balance between urban waste and wildlife. Though they look fearsome, they're surprisingly docile and are valued as quiet but effective city scavengers.

SPARKLEHOOF
(SPARKLE-HOOF)

The Sparklehoof is a captivating, tiny creature, only about an inch long, with delicate antlers and deer-like features atop its ant body. Known for its enchanting glow, the Sparklehoof illuminates the forest floor at night, using its bioluminescent antlers to communicate with others in its group.

A nocturnal scavenger, the Sparklehoof feeds on tiny plant particles and spores, playing a small but essential role in its ecosystem. Moving in small, synchronized groups, Sparklehooves create trails of light that shimmer like stars scattered across the ground, inspiring myths and folklore about "fairy pathways" in the woods. Their gentle glow serves as a natural defense, confusing some predators and allowing them to slip away into the shadows, leaving behind only their ethereal light.

ELEWHAL
(ELLA-WALL)

The Elewhal is a massive, gentle creature that roams shallow coastal waters and estuaries, resembling a cross between an elephant and a whale. Its four powerful legs allow it to wade easily through water, and its trunk is specially adapted for gathering aquatic plants, algae, and seagrass. The Elewhal's tusks help it dig through the sandy seabed or pry up dense sea vegetation for feeding.

Social and family-oriented, Elewhals travel in small pods, often communicating through low-pitched calls that resonate through the water. Despite their size and strength, Elewhals are peaceful by nature, rarely displaying aggression and instead using their sheer presence to deter potential threats. Occasionally, they'll venture onto land to graze on coastal grasses, making them as versatile as they are imposing. With their calm demeanor and fascinating mix of elephantine and aquatic traits, Elewhals are truly unique denizens of the coastal ecosystems they call home.

GATORWING
(GATE-OR-WING)

The Gatorwing is a unique predator, combining the aerial prowess of a hawk with the powerful jaws and fangs of an alligator. Soaring over rivers and swamps, the Gatorwing uses its sharp eyesight to spot prey from high above, swooping down with lightning speed to capture fish, small mammals, and reptiles.

Its powerful talons enable it to snatch prey mid-flight, while its strong jaws deliver a deadly bite. Gatorwings are solitary and fiercely territorial, often claiming a large section of river or marshland as their own. Known for their stealth and surprising agility, Gatorwings are respected as apex predators in their environment, blending the fierce agility of a hawk with the raw power of an alligator.

PINKTOOTH
(PINK-TOOTH)

The Pinktooth is a menacing creature of the deep, easily recognizable by its intense pink coloration and large, piercing eyes. With razor-sharp teeth and an angry expression, it is both an intimidating hunter and a fierce defender of its territory. Known to stalk its prey silently, the Pinktooth relies on quick bursts of speed to ambush fish and other sea creatures, using its sharp teeth to deliver a crushing bite.

This predator is not only aggressive but highly territorial, often warding off larger marine creatures that come too close to its hunting grounds. Despite its bright color, the Pinktooth blends well into coral reefs and other vibrant ocean landscapes, allowing it to ambush with stealth. Its presence in any area is enough to keep other creatures wary, as the Pinktooth is both an efficient and relentless predator.

PUFFKIN
(PUFF-KEN)

The Puffkin is a bright, striking creature, covered in vibrant blue, feathery fluff that makes it stand out in any environment. Despite its conspicuous color, the Puffkin thrives by being agile and alert, using its large eyes and quick reflexes to spot and snatch insects from branches, leaves, and even mid-air.

This social creature loves to gather in small, noisy groups, often creating a lively scene as they chatter and explore together. With no natural camouflage, Puffkins rely on their high-pitched calls to warn each other of approaching predators, quickly scattering and hiding in trees or bushes. Known for sunbathing in the open, they often playfully fluff up their feathers, becoming a memorable sight with their bright blue color, endearing ears, and lively, social behavior.

BRANCHKIN
(BRANCH-KEN)

The Branchkin is a small, six-inch creature with a brown, scaly body covered in branch-like projections, blending effortlessly into tree trunks and foliage. Despite its incredible camouflage, the Branchkin is highly sought after by predators due to its rich nutrients and soft, easily digestible body, making it ideal for feeding young offspring.

With large, endearing black eyes, the Branchkin is a harmless forager, living on a diet of insects and plants. Its sharp senses and quick reflexes help it detect nearby threats, but it mostly relies on its natural disguise to stay hidden. Living in dense forests, Branchkins play a vital role in the ecosystem, acting as a nutritious food source for many species while subtly aiding in pest control through their insect-based diet.

CAIMACAW
(CAME-UH-CAW)

The Caimacaw is a bold and colorful predator, reaching up to 8 inches in height with vivid plumage that rivals even the brightest parrots. Unlike typical parrots, this bird uses its hybrid beak—sharp and powerful, like an alligator's jaws—to hunt small animals, making it a formidable hunter despite its size.

Active and social, Caimacaws often hunt in small flocks, coordinating to take down slightly larger prey or to defend their territory. With sharp claws and an alligator-like bite, they are surprisingly strong for their size and can be quite aggressive if threatened. Their bright colors serve as a warning, signaling to potential threats that these little predators are not to be underestimated.

SHELLNECK
(SHELL-NECK)

The Shellneck is a peculiar creature, blending the protective armor of a turtle with the height and reach of a giraffe. Standing tall above ground vegetation, the Shellneck uses its long neck to nibble on leaves from branches most turtles couldn't dream of reaching. Its sturdy legs and low center of gravity make it incredibly stable, and its thick shell provides a secure retreat if threatened.

Though slow-moving, Shellnecks are well-adapted to their environment, using their long necks to stay alert for predators while browsing for food. The creature's unique form allows it to graze both high and low, making it one of the most versatile herbivores in its habitat. Known for their gentle nature, Shellnecks are highly social, often seen in small groups that graze together, creating an endearing sight with their mix of elegance and steadfastness.

TIGROD
(TIE-GRAWD)

The Tigrod is a magnificent creature with bold tiger stripes across a painted dog-like body, blending beauty with wild agility. Mostly active at dusk and dawn, Tigrods use their keen senses to navigate twilight landscapes, making them adept hunters of small mammals, birds, and even occasional fruits or roots.

Living in close-knit pairs or small groups, Tigrods maintain a semi-solitary lifestyle but will sometimes form temporary alliances with other pairs for added safety or coordinated hunting. Known for their intelligence and quiet vigilance, they take turns resting and keeping watch, creating a bond rooted in trust and cooperation. With their unique markings and graceful movements, Tigrods are as striking as they are enigmatic, representing both resilience and harmony in the wild.

PANTHERRA
(PAN-THERE-UH)

The Pantherra is a striking, elusive predator, blending the stealth of a panther with the keen vision and silent flight of an owl. Its deep black feathers, tipped in golden bronze, give it a subtle shimmer under the moonlight, making it a mesmerizing sight in the wild. With an owl-panther head that combines sharp, swiveling vision and feline precision, the Pantherra is an unrivaled night hunter.

This solitary creature patrols dense forests, relying on its quiet wing beats and powerful talons to ambush prey like small mammals and birds. The Pantherra's presence is both feared and admired, symbolizing elegance and lethal grace.

INKGUIN
(INK-GWIN)

The Inkguin is a marvel of the deep, blending the grace of a penguin with the adaptability of an octopus. With a penguin body cloaked in flowing octopus tentacles, the Inkguin glides through underwater landscapes, its "cloak" helping it blend seamlessly into coral reefs and kelp forests. The tentacles serve both as camouflage and as a defense mechanism, creating a startling display when flared to ward off potential predators.

Known for its unique hunting techniques, the Inkguin dives into deep waters to catch fish, squid, and crustaceans, using its tentacles to create a deceptive silhouette that confuses prey and predators alike. Social by nature, Inkguins often travel in small pods, where their tentacles create a mesmerizing, almost hypnotic display in the water. Admired for its intelligence and adaptability, the Inkguin is a rare and enchanting sight in its oceanic habitat.

MOSQUIPPO
(MUSK-QUIP-POE)

The Mosquippo is a daunting, blood-sucking beast that roams marshy terrains and swampy waters. Equipped with powerful mosquito-like wings, it hovers just long enough to ambush unsuspecting prey with a fierce bite. Unlike typical mosquitos, the Mosquippo uses its sharp, hippo-sized teeth to puncture the skin, drawing blood in a painful process that can break bones if it clamps down with full force.

This aggressive creature is highly territorial and will defend its marshy home fiercely, often driving off other animals with its sheer presence. Although primarily bloodthirsty, the Mosquippo supplements its diet with swamp plants, maintaining a balanced intake to fuel its energy and keep its strength. Its combination of hippo brute force and mosquito persistence makes it a true nightmare of the wetlands.

Check out our other books
by searching Inked Crown Publishing
on Google or Amazon

Literally something for everyone!

INKED CROWN
PUBLISHING

Check out our other photo books by searching Inked Crown Publishing on Amazon or Google. Again, thank you for picking up this book and sacrificing your valuable time to flip through our book.

The Creature Chronicles | 100 Beasts Born from Imagination
Copyright 2024 by Inked Crown Publishing

All rights reserved. No part of this book may be used or reproduced in any manner whatsoever without the express written permission of the publisher.

All images were created using Pikaso and human ideas.

Printed in Great Britain
by Amazon